Summer
with ELISA

Johanna Hurwitz

Summer
with ELISA

ILLUSTRATED BY
Heather Harms Maione

SCHOLASTIC INC.
New York Toronto London Auckland Sydney
Mexico City New Delhi Hong Kong

For my granddaughter—
Juliet Elizabeth Hurwitz
I wish you joy every season of the year

ISBN 0-439-28029-X

12 11 10 9 8 7 6 5 4 3 2   2 3 4 5 6/0

Printed in the U.S.A.   40

First Scholastic printing, November 2000

Contents

Summer Plans

It was the twenty-fourth of June. Two minutes ago Elisa Michaels had finished the first grade. But even though she was cheering with all the other boys and girls as they rushed happily from the building, she still wished school weren't over. She could hardly wait until September, when second grade would begin. Second grade was much more grown-up than first!

Elisa's mother was waiting outside the school

to walk her home. "You have a whole long summer vacation ahead of you," Mrs. Michaels said. "We'll have to think of some good things to keep you busy."

"Marshie, I'll be home to play with you every day," Elisa told her baby brother, whose real name was Marshall. He was being pushed along in his stroller. Marshall was only twenty months old. He still didn't say very much, but he could walk and run and follow Elisa around the house. He could dig in the sandbox at the park and build with blocks at home. Elisa thought it would be lots of fun to help take care of him during the summer.

Marshall banged on his stroller with the bagel he had been chewing. He was busy teething, and he didn't care about school and vacation time.

When they got to their apartment building, Elisa's big brother, Russell, who had his own key nowadays, was already home.

"Just four more days, and I'm off to sleepaway camp," he announced proudly.

Elisa had watched early in the month as her mother had packed and shipped off a big trunkful of clothing for Russell to wear during the three weeks he would be away from home. There were new T-shirts and new shorts, new socks and new underwear. In every piece of clothing Mrs. Michaels had attached a small label that read RUSSELL MICHAELS in bright red letters.

Elisa wished she had a trunkful of new clothing with her name on every piece, but she was glad she wasn't going away from New York City to sleepaway camp. She wouldn't like to be separated from her parents and Marshall for so long. But Russell was much bigger. He was eleven years old, so he wanted to go away. At least he *said* he wanted to go away. Elisa wondered if he really and truly meant it.

Elisa thought it would be strange not to have Russell home for three whole weeks. But in a way it would be fun too. For three weeks she would be the oldest child in the family. For three weeks Russell wouldn't be around to boss and tease her. For three weeks she and Marshall would have their parents to themselves.

"I won't get homesick," Russell told his parents confidently.

"What's homesick?" Elisa asked.

"Homesick means that you miss your home," Mr. Michaels explained to his daughter.

"Won't you miss your home?" Elisa asked Russell.

"I don't think I'll miss *you*," he said. "It will be fun to live in a cabin with a bunch of other boys who are my age. We're going to have big adventures together."

"You may feel a tiny bit homesick at first," Mrs. Michaels told Russell. "But it will pass, and then you'll be home again before you know it."

"Be sure to write to me," Russell instructed his family on the morning he was leaving for camp.

Mrs. Michaels surprised him by saying, "I already did."

"Why did you write to Russell when he's still here?" Elisa asked.

"I mailed a letter to the camp. I knew it would be fun for him to get mail as soon as he arrived."

"What did you say in it?" Russell wanted to know.

"You'll have to wait and read the letter," said Mrs. Michaels.

"I wish you'd write me a letter," Elisa said to her mother.

"Someday when you go to camp, I'll send letters to you there," her mother replied. But Elisa wasn't at all sure it would be worth going away from home for so long just to receive mail of her own.

"You write to me too, Elisa," Russell requested. "I want lots of letters."

"Okay, I will," she promised her brother. She hoped something exciting would happen so she could write about it.

As soon as Mr. Michaels took Russell to the

bus terminal, Elisa ran to get a piece of paper and a pencil. She sat down at the kitchen table and began writing. "Dear Russell," she wrote. "I hope you are having a good time at camp." She stopped to look at her words. That's silly, she thought. How can Russell be having a good time? He hasn't even gotten on the bus yet. Elisa scrunched up the paper into a ball and threw it in the garbage. She would write a letter to Russell tomorrow.

Supper without Russell wasn't too strange. It was as if he were having a sleepover at a friend's house. But when Russell didn't come home the next day, it felt different.

"I wonder what Russell's doing at camp," Elisa said to her mother.

"You could write him a letter and ask," Mrs. Michaels suggested.

Elisa pulled out a sheet of paper. "Dear Russell," she wrote. "Is camp fun? I've been having fun playing with Annie." Elisa stopped writing. Russell wouldn't care that she had gone

6

to the playground yesterday. She went to the playground all the time. She wished she had something new and special to write about. She scrunched up the paper into a ball and threw it in the garbage.

That morning Marshall was due for a checkup at the doctor's office. Elisa went along. She was glad the checkup was not for her. Instead she could watch the iguana in the waiting-room terrarium while Marshall had to get a shot. She remembered that once, when she was little, Russell told her that the iguana was going to get out of the terrarium and bite her. She had believed him and gone running to her mother for safety. Of course Russell had just been teasing her. He had always teased her, since she was as little as Marshall was now.

Elisa smiled and tapped the glass of the ter-rarium. These days it was much harder for Russell to frighten her. The iguana turned its head slightly, and Elisa stuck her tongue out at him. She knew he couldn't get out of the terrarium! Still, she sort of missed having Russell around to tease her. On some days she only pretended that she believed him. It was a game they played together.

During the following days, nothing special happened. Sometimes Elisa played with one of her classmates. Once she went to the library with her mother. She had her hair trimmed at the barbershop, and her mother bought her a pair of open sandals that she could wear without socks. None of these was anything that would interest Russell. So Elisa put off writing to him while she waited for something really important to tell.

One day, when Russell had been away at camp for almost two weeks, Elisa received a letter from her big brother.

Dear Elisa,
I am not homesick for you. I go swimming every day here. I've learned how to dive off the low board. Maybe before I come home, I'll even be able

to dive from the high board. There
are twelve boys in my bunk. Their
names are Ted, Larry, Sam, Evan,
Ethan, Noah, Bobby, Keith, Chris, Mike
K., Mike P., and me. The food stinks,
but otherwise camp is fun.

From,
Russell

P.S. keep out of my room or you'll
get in big trouble when I get home.

Elisa read the letter over and over. It wasn't
often that she got a letter. It was also exciting that
her reading skills were good enough that she
understood almost every word without help.

"The food stinks," she read aloud, giggling.
"The food stinks." *Stinks* had never been a reading word at school, but she was able to sound
it out.

Elisa had actually gone into Russell's room a
few times since he had been away. Once, just a
day or two after Russell had left for camp, she

had run into the room looking for him. At that moment she had forgotten he was away. But usually she went to look at his shelves of books and toys. She never touched anything. Russell's things just reminded her comfortingly that he would be back again. She wondered how Russell was able to guess that she had been inside.

Now that he had written to her, Elisa knew that she *must* write to him.

Dear Russell,
    I am glad I don't go to camp if the food stinks there. The food is good here. I helped Mommy make chocolate chip cookies yesterday. we had spaghetti and meatballs for supper last night. And the night before we had corn on the cob.

Elisa stopped to look at all she had written. Her mother had helped her by spelling aloud the

words *chocolate*, *yesterday*, and *spaghetti*.

Maybe Russell would get homesick if he heard about all those good foods here at home, she thought. She scrunched up her letter into a ball and threw it in the garbage. She would start again.

Dear Russell,
I am sorry that the food stinks at camp. Since you have been gone, Marshall got another tooth. Yesterday he fell in the park and hurt his knee. Mommy put a Band-Aid on it, but he pulled it off. I am fine. I am a little homesick for you even if you aren't homesick for me.
Love,
Elisa

Elisa was tired from so much writing. She folded her letter and put it inside an envelope.

Her mother had put the address of Russell's camp on the refrigerator. Elisa removed the magnet and took down the paper with the address. Carefully she copied all the information. Then she put the paper back. She got a stamp from the little box on her father's desk where he kept them. She licked the stamp and stuck it on the corner of the envelope. All she had to do now was lick the flap that closed the envelope and put it inside a mailbox.

Just as Elisa was about to do that, she had a thought. Suppose something very exciting happens later today, or tomorrow? She'd better wait to seal the envelope. Then she could add the information to her letter. Elisa put the envelope inside her library book. That way she wouldn't lose it.

That evening at supper Elisa's parents told her some big news. "Soon after Russell comes home from camp, we're going on a vacation together to the country," Mr. Michaels explained.

"To the country?" Elisa asked with wonder.

"Yes. We are renting a house with a big garden for you to play in. It will almost be as if we're living inside the park," said her mother.

"We're going to another country!" Elisa shouted. "I can't believe it."

"No, no. It's not another country," said her father. "It's our country. But it's not in the city. There will be trees and flowers and plenty of room for you to play outside. We'll have a lake nearby for swimming."

"That sure sounds like another country to me," said Elisa. "What is it called?"

"Connecticut," said Mrs. Michaels.

"I will write it in my letter to Russell," Elisa exclaimed. Finally she had some really big news to tell her brother.

When supper was over, Elisa ran to get her library book. It wasn't on her chest of drawers. She looked all over her room. "I lost my library book," she told her mother.

"Oh. Don't worry about it," said Mrs. Michaels, laughing. "I knew you'd finished read-

14

ing it, so I returned it when I took Marshall there for Toddler Time."

Elisa gasped. "You returned my book?"

"That's right," said Mrs. Michaels. "It was while you were in the playground with Annie Chu and her mother."

"But I left my letter to Russell inside it," Elisa said.

"Oh, I'm sorry. I didn't notice it. But you know what? I bet someone will find it and mail it to Russell," her mother said consolingly. "The chances are very good that he'll still get the letter from you after all."

But a week later, when Russell came home with a trophy for Most Improved Swimmer, seven mosquito bites, and a trunkful of dirty laundry, he said he'd never gotten a single letter from Elisa.

Elisa was very happy to see her big brother after all this time. But she was very sorry to hear that the letter never arrived. "I wrote a letter, but I left it in my library book," Elisa explained.

"What good is that?" Russell wanted to know. He looked taller, and he was suntanned, but he sure sounded just like the old Russell.

"It doesn't really matter," said Mrs. Michaels. "You're home now. Elisa can tell you all her news in person."

Elisa tried to think. What had she written in her letter to Russell? She couldn't remember anything at all. But she did know the one thing she hadn't written. "Russell!" she shouted. "Guess what? We're all going on a trip together. We're going to the country for our vacation."

"All of us? What fun is that?" asked Russell.

"I think you'll have a good time," Mr. Michaels told Russell. "I hope it will be just as much fun for you as camp."

"It can't be as much fun as camp," Russell told his father. "All my new friends won't be there. Just us." Then he turned to Elisa. "You'll see. Next summer, when I go back to camp, I'm not going to send you a letter."

"Please," Elisa begged him. "Pretty please."

"Next summer is a long way off," Mrs. Michaels pointed out. "I wouldn't worry about it now."

"If Elisa cared about me, she would have sent me a letter. I sent one to her."

"I can't help it if my letter was inside the library book that Mommy returned."

Mrs. Michaels leaned over and whispered something quietly in Elisa's ear.

"Secrets aren't polite," grumbled Russell. It was something he'd been told many times.

Marshall banged his spoon against his plastic dish. He didn't care about letters or secrets. But he liked to make a lot of noise.

The next morning Mrs. Michaels took Elisa to the library. At supper she had whispered that perhaps the letter Russell never received was still waiting inside the library book. Luckily Elisa remembered both the author and the title. She ran to the shelf and found the book. Inside, there was her letter, just where she had put it for safe-keeping.

"I found it!" she shouted with delight.

"Now you can give it to Russell," said Mrs. Michaels.

"Oh, no, no. I have a better idea," said Elisa excitedly.

And that is why, just one day later, Russell received a letter in the mail from his sister, with his camp address crossed out on the envelope and his home address penciled in. Elisa had mailed the letter on her way home from the library. The news in the letter was old by now, and Elisa had forgotten to add the P.S. about their trip to the country. But it didn't matter, she thought. The important thing was that Russell felt important getting a letter. It proved that his sister cared for him.

"From now on, when you write letters, you should mail them right away" was all Russell said to Elisa after he read it.

"When we go to the country, I am going to write lots of letters," Elisa said. "And then I'll go and put them in the mailbox right away," she promised.

Marshall banged his spoon on the table. He was too little to care about mailboxes and letters. He wanted more chocolate pudding.

A Pet for Elisa

Traveling to the country seemed to take forever. First there were many trips from their apartment down to the street to load the car with all of the family's suitcases. In addition to clothing, Mrs. Michaels had packed sheets and towels. Russell and Elisa were each allowed to fill a small overnight bag with other things they wanted to bring.

Russell brought his camera, a pair of binoculars, two paperback books, and a box with a new jigsaw puzzle. His parents also permitted him to bring his kite, even though it didn't fit inside the overnight bag.

Elisa brought Airmail, her old rag doll that she liked to sleep with. The other things she put inside the bag were a package of colored markers, a notebook of unlined paper for drawing, a book of paper dolls, and a pair of scissors.

Of course Marshall couldn't pack a bag, so his mother selected a few of his favorite playthings for him. Everything was squeezed into the trunk of the car. Russell and Elisa sat in the backseat with Marshall in his car seat between them.

"We each have a window," Elisa said to Russell. "But not Marshie," she added thoughtfully.

"Marshall is happy to go for a ride," said her mother. "He doesn't care where he sits." She placed a large picnic cooler on the floor of the backseat. It was filled with sandwiches and fruit and juice for them to eat along the way.

Elisa waved good-bye to their apartment building. She was sorry that none of their neighbors like Nora and Teddy Resnick or Mrs. Wurmbrand was around to see them go off. Nora and Teddy were still at their sleepaway camp, but Mrs. Resnick had offered to water the Michaelses' plants and feed Russell's fish until they returned home.

The trip took four hours. It would have taken less time, except along the way first Elisa and then Russell needed to take rest stops to go to the bathroom.

"It's a good thing Marshie wears diapers," said Elisa. "Otherwise, we'd have to make a stop for him to go to the bathroom too."

At last they pulled up in front of a white house on a road with only a few other houses and many trees nearby. "This is the place," announced Mrs. Michaels, who was holding a map.

Elisa couldn't decide if she wanted to see the outside or the inside first. But when her father opened their door of their vacation house, she

22

ran inside with the other members of her family.

Everything about the house was interesting to her—the carpeting on the floor; the furniture, which was different from theirs at home; the rooms and stairs. Imagine! They could go upstairs and downstairs inside this house. In their city apartment all the rooms were on one level. In the bathroom there was a sliding door attached to the tub instead of the shower curtain with fish on it that they had at home. Elisa opened the door and looked inside. The bathtub looked just like a bathtub, but it would be fun to be inside it with the door closed.

"Oh! There's a fireplace," Elisa shouted with excitement when she looked around the living room. "Remember how the wolf tried to climb down the chimney to catch the three little pigs?" Then she thought of something. "Are there any wolves around here?"

"No, not a single one," Mr. Michaels reassured her.

"I sure wish a wolf would come down this

chimney," Russell said. "That would be something really exciting to tell my friends when I got back home."

Upstairs there was a bedroom for Russell and one for Elisa to share with Marshall. The TV set was in the biggest bedroom, where Mr. and Mrs. Michaels would sleep.

Elisa opened all the closets, but they were empty except for the hangers. She opened the drawers in the chest in her bedroom. They were empty too. It would have been fun to find something inside, she thought.

In the kitchen Elisa examined the dishes on which they would be eating their vacation meals. She liked them. Unlike the white plates with blue and green stripes that they had at home, these dishes had pretty flowers all around the rims. Even string beans would taste good on a plate with flowers, she thought.

When Elisa finished exploring inside, she asked if they could go outdoors.

"I want to make the beds," Mrs. Michaels

said. "But if you stay nearby, you can go outside by yourself."

"Alone? I can go outdoors all alone?" Elisa asked in amazement. In the city she never went outside unless a grown-up was with her.

"It's different in the country," said Mr. Michaels, who was bringing in the last of the suitcases.

Elisa rushed outside and looked around. There was grass surrounding the house just like in the park back home, but there were no benches. They could sit right on the ground, she thought. That would be much more fun than an old bench. Back home she rarely sat on the grass. Too many people walked their dogs and didn't clean up after them. But here the grass looked very clean. Elisa sat down, and the pieces of grass tickled her bare legs.

Suddenly she saw a motion in front of her. She looked carefully. The small green creature near her was a frog. Even though she'd never seen a *real* one before, she recognized it at once. She

wasn't afraid of it at all. The next time the frog jumped, Elisa tried to catch it. The little frog was too fast for her.

Elisa didn't give up, though. Three more times the frog jumped, and twice more it got away. Elisa followed after it, and on the next jump she grabbed it in her hand. She put her other hand over the first to make a little cup. It felt funny to have a frog inside her hand, but she held it carefully, so it couldn't escape.

"Look what I found! Look what I found!" she shouted, running into the house. She opened her top hand cautiously so Russell could have a peek.

"Aw. It's only a little frog," said Russell. "Can I hold it?"

"First take our picture," demanded Elisa.

Russell ran and got his camera out of the overnight bag. "Smile," he told them.

"I wonder if frogs can smile," said Elisa. She removed her top hand so the frog was visible, and she grinned for the camera. Only after the

27

picture was taken did she let Russell hold the frog in his hands.

"Be careful. Don't let it get away," said Elisa. "I want to make it into my pet. I always wanted a pet."

"You can't have a frog for a pet," said Russell.

"Why not?" Elisa wanted to know.

Russell couldn't think of an answer, but he was sure he was right.

While Russell was holding the little frog, Elisa looked for something that could be made into a frog home. Her mother came to the rescue with a large plastic container that was meant for storing food. It was deep enough that the small frog couldn't jump out.

The container needed something more to make it a good home for a frog. Elisa took a tablespoon from the kitchen drawer and went back outside to dig up some dirt to put on the bottom of the container. She found a few small stones, and she tore up a bit of grass to put inside the container as well.

"He'll need water to drink," Russell pointed out.

"Use this," said Mr. Michaels. He handed Elisa the lid from an empty jar. It was big enough that, once it was filled with water and put inside the container, it almost looked like a small pond.

"What will he eat?" asked Elisa. She'd heard of buying cat food and dog food and fish food. But she'd never heard of frog food.

"Frogs eat bugs," said Russell.

Elisa made a face. "That's disgusting."

"Not if you're a frog," said Russell.

"Well, where can I get bugs?" she asked.

"If you leave the container outdoors, in some shady spot, bugs will probably come to the frog," suggested Mr. Michaels. That solved the feeding of Elisa's new pet.

"He needs a name," Elisa announced.

Everyone except Marshall had a name to offer.

"Prince Charming," said Mrs. Michaels.

"Kermit," said Mr. Michaels.

"How about Mike?" suggested Russell. "Then he'll be Mike Michaels."

Elisa shook her head at every idea they gave her.

"It's your frog. You found him—you name him," said Russell, shrugging.

So Elisa spent the rest of the afternoon thinking about names. She thought of the names of her favorite book characters and the names of her first-grade classmates. Finally she hit upon the perfect name. "Freddy the Frog," she announced to everyone. "That's his name."

The frog didn't pay any attention to all this. He stayed in the container without moving much. But when she watched closely, Elisa could see his chest move in and out as he was breathing. "He likes privacy," she told her family. "He doesn't want to hop around when everyone is looking at him."

Even so, Elisa could not take her eyes off her new pet. When Mr. Michaels headed for the nearest supermarket with a shopping list and he invited Elisa to join him, she didn't want to go. Freddy might start hopping or doing some other frog activity while she was away.

"Could I take Freddy with me?" she asked.

"Supermarkets have rules about bringing pets inside," said Mr. Michaels. So he went off by himself to buy all the things the family needed to fill the empty refrigerator and cupboards.

Later that evening Elisa could hardly bear to say good-night to Freddy. "Can't I bring his container into my bedroom?" she begged.

"I think he'll be happier outdoors," said her mother. "You'll see him in the morning."

Elisa had been looking forward to sleeping in her new bed, so she blew good-night kisses to Freddy and came inside the house. She had a bath in the tub with a door and got into bed.

Marshall was so pleased to see her that he stood up in the crib and began calling, "Leese, Leese." That was how he said Elisa's name.

Mrs. Michaels came into the room to kiss the children good-night. "Have a good sleep," she told them. "We'll be busy doing many things tomorrow." Then she turned out the light.

In the dark Elisa was glad to have Marshall across the room and soft, cuddly Airmail in her arms.

When Elisa woke the next morning, Airmail was on the floor and Marshall was no longer in the crib. She ran downstairs and found her mother fixing some breakfast for her little brother. "Can I go see Freddy?" Elisa begged.

"Sure," Mrs. Michaels answered. Elisa had already forgotten that her parents said things were different in the country. They certainly were. At home she never went outside in her pajamas!

The ground made Elisa's bare feet wet, but that didn't bother her. She rushed right to Freddy's home. He was sitting near the jar lid of water.

"Did you eat some bugs for your breakfast?"

she asked him, making a face. It sounded yucky to her. Toast crumbs would be so much better. She picked Freddy up and held him gently.

That day the Michaels family took a drive to see the area. The lake was nearby, and people were swimming and picnicking. Mr. Michaels said he would rent a rowboat and take the children out on the water one day soon.

They went to a nature museum with loads of real animals that had been preserved for them to admire: beavers and bears, porcupines and skunks, and many, many birds of all sizes and colors. "But they don't have a frog," Elisa pointed out. "I have a frog!"

"Big deal," said Russell.

The reunion between Elisa and Freddy at the end of the day *was* a big deal. She greeted her pet with a detailed description of all that she'd seen and done.

At suppertime, as they sat around the table in the vacation house eating hamburgers and fresh corn on the cob, Elisa began talking about where she'd keep Freddy when they returned to New York City.

"I don't think the city is a good place for a little frog," said Mrs. Michaels. "It would be better to play with Freddy now and to let him go when we return home."

"Oh no," Elisa replied. "I can't do that."

She thought about places where Marshall couldn't reach. Maybe the top of her chest of drawers in her bedroom would be the safest place for Freddy.

Four days after the Michaels family had settled into their vacation house, Elisa woke to a terrible discovery. Freddy had disappeared from the container.

"He's gone! He's gone!" She wept.

"I bet he jumped out," said Russell. "It must have been boring for him to sit in the same place day after day."

"It wasn't boring. It was his new home," Elisa

said, whimpering. She crawled along on the grass, trying to find her lost pet.

Mr. Michaels came outside to help her search. They looked through the grass and under the bushes nearby, but there was no sign of the little frog. Elisa sobbed. "I wanted to take him home with me. He was my pet. I wanted to show him to my friends and take him to school and everything."

"Elisa," said her father softly, "Freddy must have gone back to his mother and father. That's where he belongs, not inside a plastic container with a jar lid for water. It wouldn't have been right for you to take him all the way home to New York City. You wouldn't want to live so far away from Mommy and me, would you?"

Elisa sat on her father's lap and sobbed quietly into his shirt.

"Do you think he'll miss me?" she asked.

"Of course he'll miss you. But he'd miss his family even more," said Mr. Michaels.

"Maybe he has a big brother and a little

brother frog like I've got Russell and Marshie," said Elisa thoughtfully.

"Maybe he does," said her father. He pulled a tissue out of his pants pocket so Elisa could blow her nose.

"I'll always miss him," she said.

"Of course you will," he answered.

And of course she did. But it helped that during the day Mr. Michaels found a little beanbag toy in the shape of a green frog to buy for Elisa.

"I'm going to call him Freddy," she said, holding the soft toy in her hand.

"You won't have to worry about feeding this Freddy any bugs," Russell observed.

Even though Russell teased Elisa, he thought of her when he discovered a small ceramic frog in a gift shop two days later. He gave it to Elisa at suppertime.

"Is this for me?" asked Elisa delightedly.

"Of course," said Russell.

"I'm going to name him Freddy."

"What a surprise!" said Russell.

August 3

Dear Annie,

we are on a vacation.

we drove very far in our
car. It took a long time.
Russell kept teasing me. we
had two fights. Marshall
slept almost the whole way.
Mommy says she hopes all
of us will sleep on the way
back home—but not Daddy.
He has to drive the car.

Your friend,
Elisa

Up a Tree

In the country Elisa felt as if she were Little Red Riding Hood and Goldilocks and Hansel and Gretel and all the other fairy-tale characters that lived in the woods. At first she worried a bit about wolves and bears and witches in Connecticut. All the trees around the house made it easy to imagine that one of those nasty creatures might be hiding there.

"I think I just saw a wolf in the bushes," Russell would say.

The first time he said that, Elisa ran inside the house for safety.

"We would never have come here for our vacation if there were wolves," said Mr. Michaels, looking up from the newspaper he was reading.

"Maybe you didn't know about this wolf," Elisa suggested.

"Who is smarter? Russell or me?" he asked his daughter.

"You!" said Elisa.

"In that case, take my word for it. There are no wolves here." He smiled at Elisa. "Do you think Russell would have stayed outside if he thought there really was a wolf in the bushes?"

Elisa laughed. Her father was right.

"Russell likes to tease you. It's the way big brothers act," Mrs. Michaels reminded Elisa.

"I'm a big sister, and I don't tease Marshie," Elisa pointed out. Since he had come home from

40

camp, she noticed that Russell seemed worse than ever. Besides teasing all the time, he liked to brag and show off.

"I can eat three ears of corn," he boasted at suppertime. Elisa couldn't eat more than one ear. "I can stay up later than you," he gloated when Elisa had to get ready for bed that evening. Now that she was going into second grade, it didn't seem fair.

The next day at lunch Russell continued to brag. "Be sure to put mustard on my sandwich," he instructed his mother. "Mustard used to tickle my tongue, but at camp we all ate mustard. Now I love it," he said. "Babies don't like mustard," he added, looking at Elisa.

Elisa didn't like mustard. It was worse than tickling on her tongue. It burned. But she didn't want to let Russell know that. "Marshie doesn't like mustard. But I do," she said. "Put some on my sandwich too," she told her mother.

"Are you sure?" asked Mrs. Michaels.

"Yes," said Elisa. "Just a little." Maybe if she ate a little every day, her tongue would get used to it.

"I want *a lot* of mustard. I love it!" said Russell.

"I love it too," said Elisa. "I could eat a whole jar of it."

"You could not."

"Yes, I could."

"Could not."

"Could."

"I'm going to buy you a jar of mustard, just for yourself. I want to watch you eat it with a spoon," said Russell.

"No one eats mustard with a spoon," said Mrs. Michaels.

"Elisa said she could eat a whole jar, so I'm going to buy one for her," Russell insisted.

Elisa drank a lot of apple juice with her bologna sandwich to cool her tongue from the burning taste of the mustard. She didn't know how she was going to eat a whole jar just to show

42

Russell that he didn't know everything.

Because it looked as if it would rain, the family hadn't made any plans that day. Elisa didn't mind. Vacationing in the country was a big enough plan for her. But Russell was restless. He sat on the step outside the house complaining. "I can't fly my kite because there's not enough wind. I finished one of my books, and I'm saving the second one. I don't know what to do."

"You could take some pictures with your camera," Elisa suggested.

"There's nothing special to take pictures of," he told her.

"We could play checkers or a card game together," she offered.

"Boring," said Russell. He looked around. "I know what," he said. "I'm going to climb a tree. I climbed some trees when I was at camp. It's a lot of fun. You get high up, and you can see far off. And you feel like you're a bird or a squirrel," he added.

Russell looked at the trees around the house

and selected a fat one nearby. It was much taller than the house. Elisa watched with amazement as he began climbing .

"Won't you fall down?" Elisa shouted up to him anxiously.

"Not if I hold on tight," Russell called back. Already he was on a limb far over her head.

"Russell, Russell! Come back," Elisa called. She could hardly see her brother now because there were so many leaves hiding him. She began to worry. Elisa knew there were no wolves and bears and witches here in Connecticut. But maybe if Russell climbed really high, he'd enter a magic kingdom like in "Jack and the Beanstalk" and there'd be a giant waiting to eat him up. Elisa wasn't certain that she believed in giants, but she didn't like her brother to take dangerous chances.

"Russell. Please, please come back," she called again.

"Okay, okay. Here I come," said Russell.

Slowly he began to descend from the tree. Then he jumped down and brushed himself off. "That was fun," he said.

"It looks hard," said Elisa.

"It's hard if you're just a little girl. But it's easy for me," Russell bragged.

"I'm not a *little* girl," Elisa protested.

Russell laughed at his sister. "Even if you were big, you couldn't climb this tree," he told her. "There are lots of things boys can do and girls can't."

"I don't believe it," said Elisa. "Girls can do anything boys can do," she insisted. "I'll show you right now."

She went over to the tree that Russell had just climbed. "I'll climb this tree too."

"Hey, Elisa, you'd better not," said Russell nervously. He suddenly remembered how a few years ago he had dared Elisa to jump off the chest of drawers in their apartment back home and she had broken her arm.

45

"I can do it if I want," said Elisa.

"No, you can't," Russell said. "You'll get hurt, and I'll get blamed."

"You're just saying that because you want to be the only one to climb trees around here. But I can do it too," said Elisa. She tried to hoist herself up the trunk of the tree the way she had seen Russell do. It wasn't easy at all. But there was a small branch growing out of the tree that was low enough for her to stretch her leg and put her foot on. Then she put her foot onto another branch. It was sort of like climbing stairs or a ladder.

"Come on down, Elisa," Russell shouted to her.

"You went lots higher," Elisa shouted back.

"I'm lots older," Russell reminded her. But it was the wrong thing for him to tell his sister. She was more determined than ever to climb just as high as he had gone.

Then Elisa looked down. It was scary. If she looked up, she was okay, but looking down made her worry about falling. She put her leg over a

tree limb and sat hugging the trunk of the tree. Climbing up hadn't been so hard after all. But she realized that it was going to be tough work to climb down.

"Come on down," Russell called to her again.

"I'm not ready," said Elisa.

"Come on down before you fall!" Russell yelled.

The door to the house opened, and Mr. Michaels came out. "What's going on?" he asked Russell. "I could hear you shouting from inside. Marshall is taking a nap, so it would be a good idea to keep your voices down."

"Okay," said Russell.

"Hi, Daddy," a voice called from the tree.

"Elisa? Where are you?" asked her father.

"Here I am. I can see you. Can't you see me?"

Mr. Michaels looked around. Then he looked up. "Elisa Michaels," he shouted when he spotted her, "get down here on the ground at once!"

"Don't shout, Daddy. You'll wake Marshall," Russell said.

"Never mind Marshall. Elisa, how did you get up there?"

"I climbed, just like Russell," she called down to him.

"Russell, did you dare Elisa to climb this tree?" asked Mr. Michaels.

"No, I didn't! It was her own idea," said Russell. "I even told her not to climb up there."

"Well, Elisa, I'm telling you to climb down now," said Mr. Michaels.

"I can't," Elisa said softly.

"What do you mean you can't?"

"I'm scared. I'm scared I'm going to fall."

"Don't look down," said Russell. "Just put your feet on the limbs the way you did going up. But don't look at the ground."

"I'm scared."

"I'll come get you," offered Russell.

"No, you won't," shouted Mr. Michaels. "Those limbs can't hold the weight of both of you. I wish we had a ladder," he said, sighing. "Russell, you watch Elisa and I'll run down the road and see if the people at the next house have a ladder we can borrow."

He returned a few minutes later without a ladder. "No one was home there," he said.

Elisa began to cry. "I don't want to stay here forever," she said.

"Elisa, you made it up there. I bet you could make it down again," Mr. Michaels told her.

"I'll catch you if you fall," Russell promised.

"Don't scare her more than she is already," Mr. Michaels whispered to his son. "Wait a minute, Elisa. I have a new plan."

Mr. Michaels ran into the house and returned holding two sofa cushions. Then he ran back and got two more.

"I can't believe it," said Mrs. Michaels, following him and holding the cushions from the living room chair. "I turn my head for one minute, and you're up a tree."

"It was easy going up," said Elisa, sobbing, "but it's hard coming down."

"I felt a drop of rain," said Russell.

"I'm going to get all wet," said Elisa.

"Not if you come down," said Mr. Michaels encouragingly. "Turn around and put your right leg on the limb that's underneath you. Look at the tree trunk, not at the ground."

"The cushions are going to get soaked," said Russell.

"Hush," said Mrs. Michaels. "Who cares about wet cushions? Come on, Elisa. You can do it."

Elisa held on to the rough bark of the tree trunk as she managed to turn and face the tree. She put her right foot down on the limb beneath her.

"Thata girl!" shouted Mr. Michaels. The rain was coming down a bit harder now. "Now put your left foot on the next limb. You can do it."

Elisa's face was all wet. She didn't know if it was rainwater or tear water. She sniffed hard and put her left leg down.

"You're halfway down now!" shouted Russell. "Come on. Keep going."

51

From inside the house there came a loud cry. Marshall had awakened from his nap.

Usually Mrs. Michaels would have responded by going and picking up her young son. Today she didn't even seem to notice. "Come on, honey," she called.

Elisa put her foot on the limb below.

Elisa's father encouraged her. "You've almost made it."

Elisa looked down. She saw all the cushions lined up to soften the ground. The earth didn't look so far away anymore either. Carefully she put her foot on the next branch. One more, and she was practically down. She let go of the tree trunk with her right hand and wiped it on her jeans.

"Here I come," she shouted, and she jumped onto the cushions. She landed with a soft thud.

Mrs. Michaels gave her a big wet hug. Then everyone grabbed cushions off the ground and rushed inside with them. Marshall had a wet dia-

per, but everyone else was wet all over and had to change into dry clothes.

Afterward, while Marshall was sitting in the booster seat drinking milk from his training cup and eating a cookie, Mrs. Michaels went to get her hair dryer. This time it wasn't for drying her hair. She aimed it at the sofa and chair cushions to dry them.

Russell told Elisa that he'd play a game of checkers with her.

"Good," she said. "Checkers is more fun than climbing trees."

"It's a whole lot safer," said Mr. Michaels.

"And drier," added his wife.

"Not if you play checkers outdoors in the rain," said Elisa.

"But we're not," said Russell as he double-jumped his little sister.

August 4

Dear Nana and Granpa,

    Today I climbed up a tree.
    I also made a bet with Russell. I said I could eat a whole jar of musterd. Russell bet me a dollar that I could not do it. He bought a jar at the supermarket. But guess what?! I never said I would eat all that musterd IN ONE DAY. Every time Mommy makes sandwiches, I am going to put a tiny bit of musterd on mine. When the jar is all finished, Russell is going to owe me a dollar. Ha, ha on him!

Love,
Elisa

P.S. Too bad it's going to take such a long time to get the dollar.

At the Beach

One day instead of going to swim at the lake, Elisa and her family took a longer drive to Ocean Beach.

"Have I ever been to the beach before?" Elisa asked as they were getting into the car.

"When you were a little girl," her mother replied.

"As little as Marshie?" asked Elisa, pointing to her small brother, who was already strapped into

56

his car seat and busily trying to untie the laces on his sneakers.

"Marshall is twenty-one months old," said Mrs. Michaels. She counted on her fingers. "You were over three or four years old when you went to the beach."

"I don't remember," Elisa said.

"I do," chimed in Russell. "I made a castle out of sand, and you knocked it down."

"You're just making that up," said Elisa. She turned to her mother. "Did I knock down Russell's sand castle?"

"Could be," replied Mrs. Michaels. "It's the sort of thing little sisters do."

"Sure. And today if I make a sand castle, Marshall will knock it down," said Russell, sounding annoyed before anything bad had happened at all.

Luckily Mr. Michaels came out of the house carrying the big cooler with the family's lunch. He put the cooler on the floor of the backseat, just under where Elisa was sitting. Then he

57

checked that both Russell and Elisa had put on their seat belts.

"We're off," he announced as he got into the front seat next to Mrs. Michaels.

"What else happened at the beach?" Elisa asked.

"You waded in the water," Mrs. Michaels informed her.

"And you splashed me all over," Russell told her.

"Did not."

"Did too."

"You're just making it up. Mommy? Did I splash Russell when we went to the beach?" Elisa wanted to know.

"I can't remember," said Mrs. Michaels, turning around to face her children in the backseat. "But it's possible. Anyhow, splashing is part of going to the beach. You're wearing a bathing suit, so it's fine to get wet."

"What else happens at the beach?" Elisa asked.

"You can look for shells," her mother told her. "Sometimes you can find wonderful seashells along the water's edge."

"Last time I had a whole pile of shells, and Elisa threw them into the ocean," Russell remembered aloud.

"Did not."

"Did too."

"You're just making that up," Elisa protested again. She didn't think that she would ever have done *all* those bad things to Russell.

"Elisa is older now, and Marshall is too young to get into much mischief," Mrs. Michaels reassured Russell. "I'm sure everyone is going to have a great time today. We're lucky that it's such a beautiful, sunny, perfect-for-going-to-the-beach sort of day."

Elisa nodded.

"We'll see," said Russell.

"Why don't you just look out the window now and watch the scenery?" suggested Mr. Michaels.

"Okay," said Elisa. "Are we almost there yet?"

"It won't be long," said Mrs. Michaels.

Before they even saw the beach, the fresh, salty smell of the ocean came in through the car's open windows. Then Elisa gave a shout. "I see it!"

They had to drive for several more minutes until they reached the beach entrance. Mr. Michaels paid the admission fee and drove to the crowded parking area.

"There are millions of cars!" Elisa proclaimed. "Will there be room for us?"

"The beach is very big," Mrs. Michaels said. "There will be room for everyone."

"Don't forget anything," Russell called out as he jumped from his seat.

Mrs. Michaels took Marshall. Mr. Michaels took the lunch cooler. Elisa took her shovel and pail; Russell took the blanket to spread on the sand. Everyone, except Marshall, had something to carry.

"Who will carry the towels?" asked Mrs. Michaels.

"We can each put one over our shoulders," Russell suggested.

"Great plan!" said his father, patting Russell on the back.

Finally they were ready to walk onto the beach. The sand squished between Elisa's toes through her open sandals. It was finer than the sand in the park back home, and paler. Even though there were so many, many people walking all over it, the sand looked cleaner too.

They walked past other families who had spread out their blankets and towels. They walked around children digging tunnels in the sand, teenagers throwing balls and Frisbees, and adults sleeping in the sun. At last they found a spot that seemed just right.

Mr. Michaels put down the cooler and helped Russell open the big blanket. Then Mrs. Michaels put Marshall right in the center and sat down beside him. Elisa began pulling off her clothing. Underneath her shorts and T-shirt she was wearing her new green bathing suit.

"Don't move until I put suntan lotion on you," her mother instructed. So Elisa had to wait.

First Mrs. Michaels put lotion on Marshall. It must have tickled him because he laughed as she rubbed the white cream on his arms and legs.

Mr. Michaels went off and returned with a big umbrella he had rented. "Let's be careful not to get too much sun," he told his family.

Because Russell was so grown-up, he was allowed to run into the water by himself. Elisa had to wait until her father walked down to the water's edge with her. She didn't mind. There were so many people around that she worried just a little that she could get lost. All those families, all those blankets, all those umbrellas looked very much the same. Probably they all had peanut butter and jelly sandwiches inside their coolers too.

Now, without her sandals on, the sand felt hot under the soles of her feet. But when Elisa and her father reached the point where the water washed against the sand, it felt cool and damp. A small wave lapped the edge of the shore and splashed Elisa's toes. Then a second and bigger wave came, and the water reached her ankles.

"This is fun!" Elisa told her father.

The two of them walked into the water until Elisa was wet all the way up to her middle. The ocean was so exciting that Elisa didn't care that it was freezing cold.

After a while, when Elisa's teeth started chattering, they returned to the blanket. Marshall was sleeping under the umbrella, and Mrs. Michaels was reading a book.

"Your turn," Elisa's father said as he took a towel and rubbed Elisa to warm her up. Mrs. Michaels closed her book.

"See you in a few minutes," she said, and walked off toward the water.

Elisa sat down on the blanket. "Where's Russell?" she asked her father.

"He's probably made a new friend or two," Mr. Michaels said, lying back on the blanket.

Elisa picked up her shovel and started digging

in the sand. She wished Russell were there to dig with her. He might spend half his time picking on her, but it was still more fun to be with him than to play on her own. So every minute or so Elisa stopped and tried to find her brother among all the other children she saw on the beach. Russell was wearing bright red swimming trunks. But about a hundred other boys were wearing red trunks too.

Then Elisa spotted him. He was walking by himself and picking up shells.

"I see Russell," she announced with delight. "Can I go to him?"

"All right," Mr. Michaels said. "But do *not* go in the water. Okay?"

"Okay," Elisa said, nodding.

She jumped up from the blanket and made her way toward Russell. But when she got closer to him, she realized that the dark-haired boy with red trunks who she thought was her brother was actually someone else. Elisa stopped short and looked around. She saw another boy who looked

64

like Russell and ran toward him. Oh, dear. That wasn't Russell either.

Suddenly someone put a hand on her shoulder. Elisa swung around, startled, only to discover that the someone was none other than her brother.

"What are you doing walking around all alone?" Russell asked.

"I'm not alone. I'm with you," Elisa answered. Then she added, "I thought I saw you, but it was someone else."

"You want to take a walk with me?" Russell asked.

"Sure," said Elisa.

"Look," said Russell, pointing off toward their left. "That part of the beach has hardly any people. Let's go that way."

So Russell and Elisa walked along together, passing children digging tunnels, teenagers throwing balls and Frisbees, and grown-ups sleeping in the sun. But after a bit there were no blankets on the ground and fewer people around.

66

The sand was coarser, and there were more pebbles underfoot.

"It hurts my feet," Elisa complained.

"Don't be a sissy," Russell told her.

"I bet the reason there aren't any people here is that no one wants to walk on all these stones," Elisa said.

"They're all sissies," Russell said.

Elisa looked back in the direction from which they had come. It seemed a long way to the blanket with her parents and Marshall and the cooler with their lunch.

"I'm hungry," Elisa said.

"It's too early for lunch," said Russell, moving ahead.

"It is not."

"Yes, it is."

They came to a large trash can. There were strange noises coming out of the can. Russell and Elisa approached cautiously.

"What do you think it is?" Elisa asked nervously.

Russell shrugged his shoulders. Elisa thought he looked a little bit scared too.

"Do you want to look inside?" Elisa whispered.

"Sure," said Russell. He moved very quietly toward the can and peeked inside.

"Oh, look!" he shouted to his sister.

Elisa came forward slowly. She was still a little frightened of the can's contents, but she was curious too. She peeked inside and was amazed by what she saw. There was a large seagull inside the trash can.

"He must have flown inside to reach some food," Russell said. "But he can't get out."

"Why not?" asked Elisa.

"Because he can't open his wings inside the can," Russell told her.

"Will you pull him out?" Elisa asked.

"Sure," said Russell. Then he looked at the seagull again, and he paused. "His beak looks pretty strong," he said.

"Are you afraid he'll bite you?" Elisa asked.

"Oh, no," said Russell. "But maybe I'll hurt him when I try to pick him up."

"He'll be so happy to get out of the can he won't care if you hurt him," Elisa said.

"He might be happy afterward, but he'll be scared and angry first," Russell responded.

The seagull let out a loud squawk, and both Russell and Elisa jumped away.

"Maybe it *is* lunchtime," Russell said.

"You said it was too early," Elisa reminded him.

"I could have been wrong. I'm feeling hungry now too," Russell said.

"We can't leave the seagull. If no one comes to let him out of that can, he'll die in there," said Elisa.

"I know," Russell said softly.

"I know what!" Elisa shouted suddenly. "We can tip the can over. Then the seagull can get out by himself."

"Right!" Russell exclaimed. "I was going to say the same thing myself."

The trash can was very heavy. It took all of Elisa's and Russell's strength to tip it over. Finally it crashed to the ground with a loud thud.

A moment later the seagull came walking out. He strutted a bit on the ground before letting out a loud cawing sound and flying off.

"We saved him!" Elisa said.

"Yeah! We did!" Russell agreed.

Walking back toward the blanket, Elisa was so excited about saving the seagull that she didn't even notice the pebbles cutting into her feet. She didn't notice the beach attendant who approached them either.

"Hey, you kids," he called out. "I saw what you did."

"You did?" asked Russell.

"Yes. We want to keep the beach clean. Did you know that knocking over trash cans is punishable by a large fine?" the man asked in an angry voice.

"We don't have any money to pay a fine," said Russell.

"Anyhow, we didn't do anything bad," said Elisa indignantly. "We did something *fine*. We rescued a seagull that was stuck inside the trash can."

"That's right. He was trapped in there," Russell told the man.

The beach attendant paused for a moment, then nodded, "That's all right then," he said. "We don't want the seagulls to come to harm."

"We rescued him," said Elisa.

"Good work," the beach attendant said, smiling. Then he turned and walked away.

"I was more scared of him than of the noise in the trash can," Russell admitted.

"He's not a real policeman," Elisa pointed out. "He didn't even have a gun."

"Besides, we didn't do anything bad," said Russell.

The sand grew smoother, and soon they were back in the crowded area of the beach again.

"Where in the world were you?" Mr. Michaels asked when the two of them reached the blanket.

"We took a walk," Russell explained.

"We rescued a seagull," said Elisa.

"In fact, we're heroes," Russell said.

"And we're hungry too," said Elisa.

So they sat down and ate their peanut butter and jelly sandwiches and told the whole story to their parents.

They drank lemonade and smiled at each other. "It's a good thing you were with me," Russell said to his sister. "It was hard work tipping over that trash can."

"I know," said Elisa.

After lunch Russell and Elisa made a sand castle together. Elisa was much too grown-up to knock it down, and just as their mother had predicted, Marshall was too young to be a nuisance.

It was a wonderful day for all the Michaels family. And for the seagull too.

Dear Nora and Teddy,

Did you come home from camp yet?

We are having a good time in the country. It is almost like staying in a house in Riverside Park. There are hundreds of trees, chipmunks, birds, a frog (I caught him, but he got away), and a snake (I didn't want to catch him).

The best thing about the country is that we can go outdoors by ourselves. But the second day I got into big trouble. I took a walk and picked some flowers for Mommy. There were all different colors. Later a lady came to our house and scolded because I had picked the

best flowers from her garden.
I didn't know they belonged
to her.

I was very sorry to do
something so bad. But I made
a big picture of the flowers,
using all my markers. It was
the best drawing I ever made.
I brought it to the lady's
house. She gave me a hug and
said she was going to hang up
my picture so she would have
flowers all year long.

Love,
Elisa

It's Raining,
It's Pouring

The summer vacation was passing quickly. There were so many things to do in the country. Some days they went swimming at the lake. One day they drove to a petting farm. The children had a chance to see farm animals close up and to touch them. Russell tried milking a goat, and Elisa found an egg hidden in the hay of the chicken house. She was disappointed to learn that the egg wasn't hers to keep.

"I bet they hide the same eggs over and over," said Russell.

"How could a chicken do that?" Elisa asked her brother.

"Not the chickens, silly. The people who own the farm. They want you to find an egg, so they hide some in the hay."

Even though she had to turn in the egg, Elisa had a good time at the petting farm. She had never touched a cow or a horse before. She'd never seen a real live pig, or chickens, except on TV or in the movies.

Another day, just before their vacation was over, they went to an amusement park. Elisa rode on the merry-go-round. Even Marshall went on the merry-go-round. He sat with their mother and laughed and laughed the whole time.

"Merry-go-rounds are for babies," Russell claimed. He went with Mr. Michaels on the Ferris wheel.

"Do you want to come too?" their father asked Elisa. "There's room for you in the seat."

"Oh, no," said Elisa. She would love to go home and tell her friends that she had been on the Ferris wheel, but it wasn't worth the scare of actually doing it so she could talk about it afterward. She would just have to tell everyone about all the other things she had done in the country instead. Elisa stayed below and watched with awe as her father and brother got higher and higher in the sky. She was very relieved when they were safely back on the ground again.

"What are we doing tomorrow?" Russell asked as they were driving back to their house.

"Tomorrow's our last day," said Mrs. Michaels. "Then it's back to the city for all of us."

"I thought we'd take a nice ride in the car," said Mr. Michaels. "There's a waterfall about an hour away, and it's supposed to be very dramatic."

"What's a waterfall?" Elisa wanted to know.

"Don't you know anything?" Russell asked her. "It's water rushing down a mountain, sort of like a big faucet that's turned on and never turned off."

"I never saw a waterfall," said Elisa. "Did you?" she asked her brother.

"I saw it in a movie," said Russell. He shrugged his shoulders. "It's not such a big deal."

"Well, it's something Mommy and I would enjoy," said Mr. Michaels. "I thought we'd pack a picnic and have a relaxing last day in the country before we return home."

"What kind of sandwiches?" asked Russell.

"Whatever you like," said his mother. "We'll stop at the supermarket on the way to the house. I can buy cold cuts or whatever you want."

"Fry! Fry!" shouted Marshall, remembering the french fries he had eaten at lunchtime in the amusement park.

"We can't have french fries, silly," Elisa told her little brother. "They'd get cold in the cooler."

The next morning the sky was very gray. "It looks like it's going to rain," Russell announced.

"Maybe it will clear up," his mother called from the kitchen. She was already making the picnic lunch: roast beef on rolls for Russell and his father, tuna fish for Elisa and herself, a cheese sandwich for Marshall, and chocolate chip cookies for everyone.

"Don't forget the grapes," said Elisa.

"I won't."

Mr. Michaels opened the door and walked outside. "It sure looks like rain," he said.

"Maybe it will shower and clear up," said his wife hopefully.

"We could still go even if it's raining," suggested Elisa. "We could eat our picnic in the car."

"How can you see a waterfall in the rain?" Russell asked. "It won't look special if water is falling *everywhere*. We can stay home and watch TV."

"No TV," said Mrs. Michaels, shutting the cooler with all the food inside.

"Finish up your breakfast, and then you can write some postcards. Maybe by the time you finish, the weather will have improved," said Mr. Michaels.

Elisa wrote a postcard to old Mrs. W., their

neighbor back home. And then she wrote a letter to her friend Annie Chu. Russell wrote to his two best friends from school. "How many *r*'s in *Ferris*?" he called out. Elisa knew just what he was writing when she heard that.

By the time they finished their cards, it had begun to rain.

Elisa rushed to the window to look out. First the rain came down gently, but it seemed to get harder and harder the longer she looked.

"This doesn't look like a good day for our drive," Mr. Michaels admitted when he joined her at the window.

"Good," said Russell. "I didn't really want to go see an old waterfall anyhow."

"I did," said Elisa.

"Then keep looking out the window," Russell replied. "That's a waterfall out there too."

"Well, at least lunch is all ready whenever we are," said Mrs. Michaels.

"I know," said Elisa. "We could still have a picnic."

"Big deal," commented Russell. "We're going to eat sandwiches for lunch and call it a picnic. Yippee."

"We won't sit at the table," Elisa informed him. "We'll pretend we're outdoors. And we'll take the blanket and spread it on the floor and sit on it. Just like we were outside."

"Outside. Outside!" Marshall crowed happily.

"That sounds dumb. Where will we put the blanket?" Russell asked grumpily.

"Daddy. Get the cooler," Elisa instructed her father.

"How about saying please?" he reminded her.

"Please get the cooler," Elisa said. "And, Russell, please get the blanket. And, Mommy, you can hold Marshall's hand. And I'll lead the way. We'll pretend we're walking in the woods."

"Boy, this is really dumb," said Russell as they all lined up.

"Be a sport, Russell," said Mr. Michaels.

Elisa led the way. First she walked through the kitchen area. Then she walked into the living room–dining room space. All her family followed behind. Next Elisa went up the stairs to the big bedroom where her parents slept. This took a while, as Marshall was still perfecting his stair-climbing skills.

"I wonder what the name of this mountain is," Mrs. Michaels said.

"It must be Staircase Mountain," her husband responded.

When they reached the bedroom, Elisa said, "I see a hill." She pointed to the center of the room.

"It sure looks like a bed to me," said Russell.

Elisa ignored his comment and moved on. She left the bedroom and walked into the room where she and Marshall slept. "Look at those beautiful trees," she said, pointing to a painting of evergreens that hung on one wall.

"It sure looks—," Russell began, but his father gave him a poke.

"Like trees," Russell concluded.

Elisa turned and went to the bathroom.

Everyone crowded inside with her. In the bathroom she turned on the faucet in the sink.

"Look!" she exclaimed. "There's a waterfall."

"Well, so it is," agreed Mrs. Michaels. "It's not quite as big as Niagara Falls or even the falls we were originally planning to visit. But it certainly is a waterfall."

"Too bad they don't sell picture postcards here," said Russell.

Elisa turned off the faucet. "Follow me," she told her family.

They went back down Staircase Mountain and into the living room–dining room area. "This looks like a perfect spot for a picnic!" Elisa exclaimed. "Let's spread our blanket here."

"This is nuts," Russell muttered. Still, he opened the blanket and spread it on top of the carpet.

"This is a lovely spot you picked, Elisa," said Mrs. Michaels as they all sat down. "Look at that beautiful green bush over there." She pointed to the green armchair across the way.

"I'd rather sit in that bush," said Russell, getting up.

"No. It might be full of thorns or prickles," said Mr. Michaels, grabbing hold of his son and pulling him back down again.

Mrs. Michaels opened the cooler to remove all their sandwiches for lunch.

"May I have a napkin?" Mr. Michaels asked his wife.

Mrs. Michaels looked inside the cooler. "Oh, dear," she exclaimed. "I forgot to pack the napkins."

"I'll go get them," her husband said, putting his sandwich down and standing up.

"Daddy, we're in the woods. There are no napkins in the woods," Elisa shouted.

"Oh, I forgot," Mr. Michaels said, and sat down again.

Russell let out a snicker. "I hope no one has to go to the bathroom here in the woods."

"More. More," Marshall called out. He had

eaten his quarter sandwich and was ready for the next segment.

"I love tuna fish sandwiches in the woods," said Elisa, chewing happily on her lunch.

"Roast beef tastes good anywhere," said Russell.

They ate their sandwiches, and the grapes and the chocolate chip cookies. Russell and Elisa and Marshall drank apple juice while their parents drank iced tea.

"Now what?" asked Russell when all the food was consumed. "Can we go *home* now?"

"It's too early," said Elisa. "Let's play some games. And tell stories."

So they played I Spy and Animal, Vegetable, Mineral. Then Mr. Michaels told them a story about the time he went on a picnic when he was a little boy and how he'd gotten lost.

"I wish I could get lost on this picnic," Russell said.

Mrs. Michaels remembered a picnic that

she'd gone on when she was young when the food had gotten lost.

"How could you lose the food?" Elisa asked.

"Everyone thought someone else had brought it. And when we sat down to eat, there was nothing except a roll of Life Savers that my aunt Virginia had inside her pocketbook."

"What did you do then?" asked Russell.

"We all pretended that we weren't hungry. But after about half an hour we all got into the car and drove to the nearest restaurant we could find."

"Well, that proves that this was a great picnic," Elisa said. "No one got lost, and we had real food to eat."

"We could still get in the car and go for a little drive," suggested Mr. Michaels.

"Aw, Dad, that waterfall just isn't going to look very special in the rain," Russell protested.

"You're absolutely right," his father agreed. "I was thinking about a shorter ride. Who'd like to go to the ice-cream shop in town? I thought there might be some people on this picnic who would enjoy an end-of-vacation-didn't-we-have-a-good-time ice cream."

"I would!" shouted Russell, jumping up at once.

"Me too!" shouted Elisa.

"Me too!" shouted Marshall.

They gathered together all the trash from the picnic and put it inside the cooler. Russell and Elisa and Marshall put on their rain slickers, and they all made a run for the car.

"That was a pretty good picnic," said Mr. Michaels as they drove along in the rain toward the ice-cream shop.

"There was just one thing missing," said Elisa.

"Napkins," said Russell.

"No," said Elisa, shaking her head. "Something else."

"What was that?" asked their mother.

"Bugs," said Elisa. "You're supposed to have bugs at a picnic.

Dear Annie,

Tomorrow we are going home. I'll tell you all about our vacation when I see you. I'll show you the picture Russell took of me with my pet frog before the frog went away. Vacations are loads of fun, but I'm glad I'm going home. I love home the best.

Your friend,
Elisa